The Secret Circus

JOHANNA WRIGHT

A NEAL PORTER BOOK
ROARING BROOK PRESS
NEW YORK

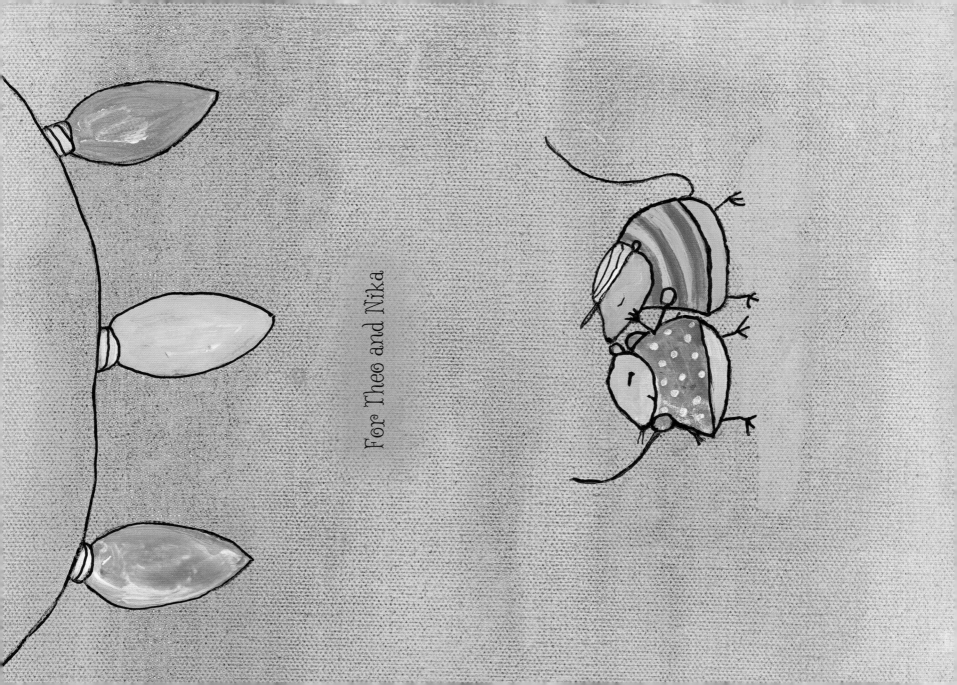

For Theo and Nika

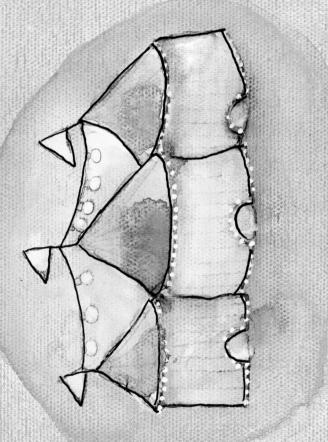

Somewhere, deep in the city of Paris, there is a circus that is so small, and so secret . . . .

only the mice
know how to find it.

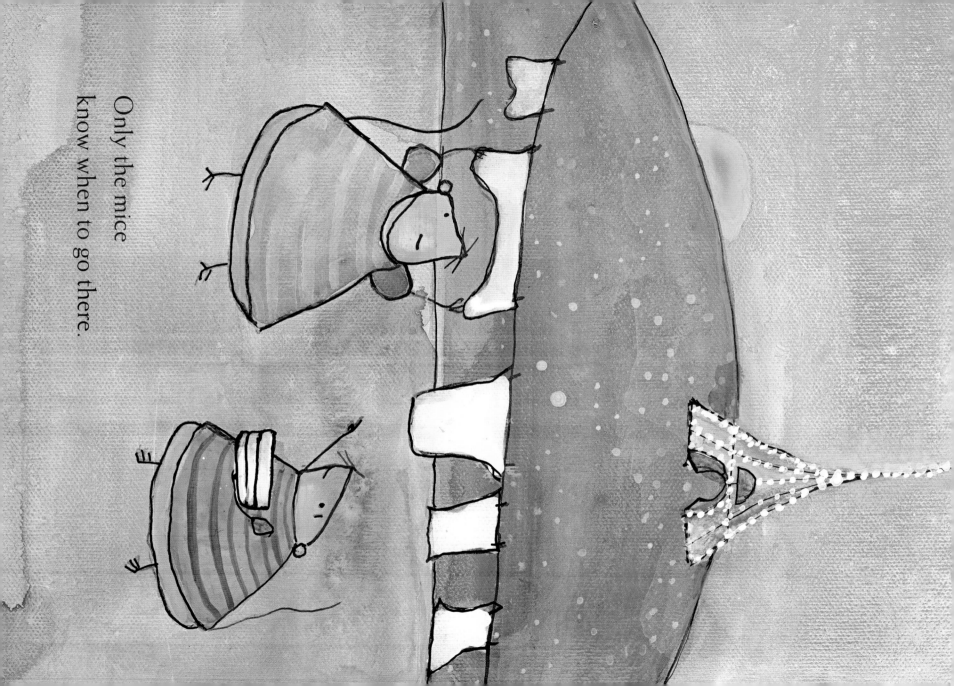

Only the mice
know when to go there.

Only the mice know what to wear.

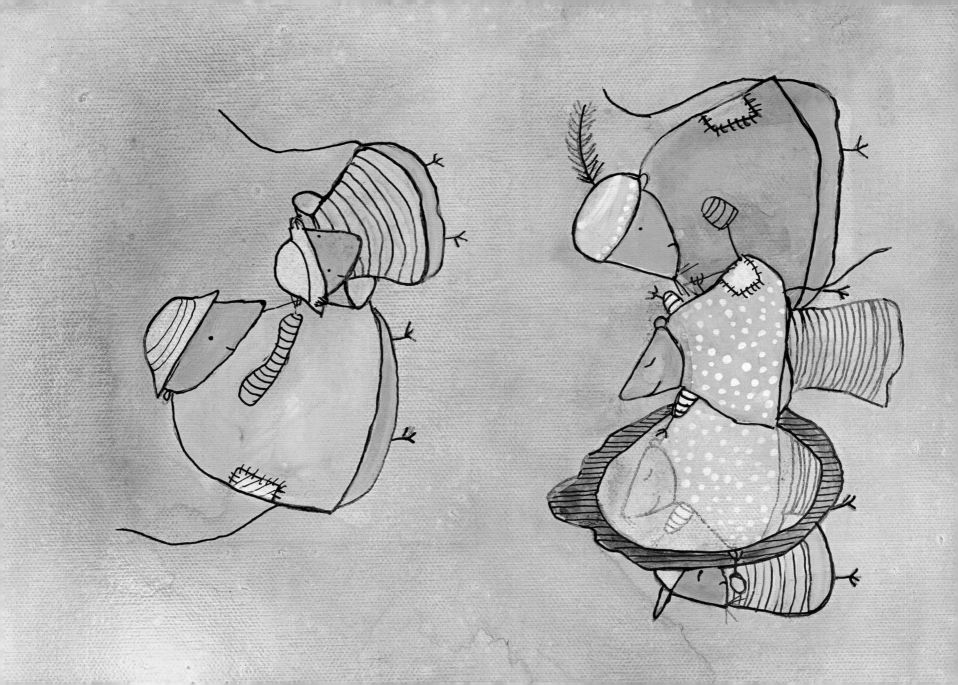

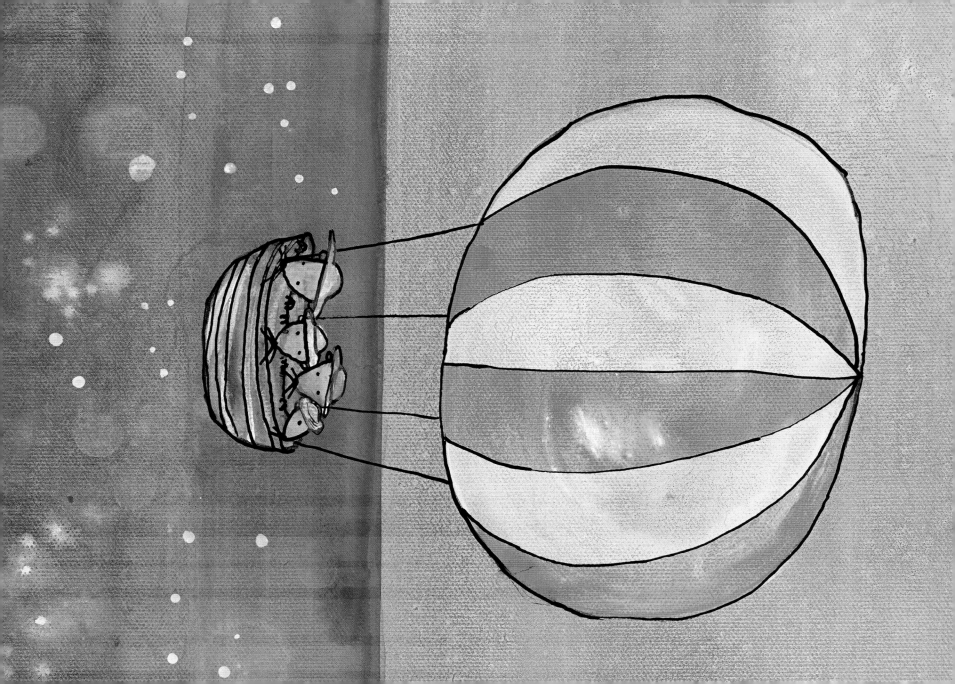

Only the mice know how to get there.

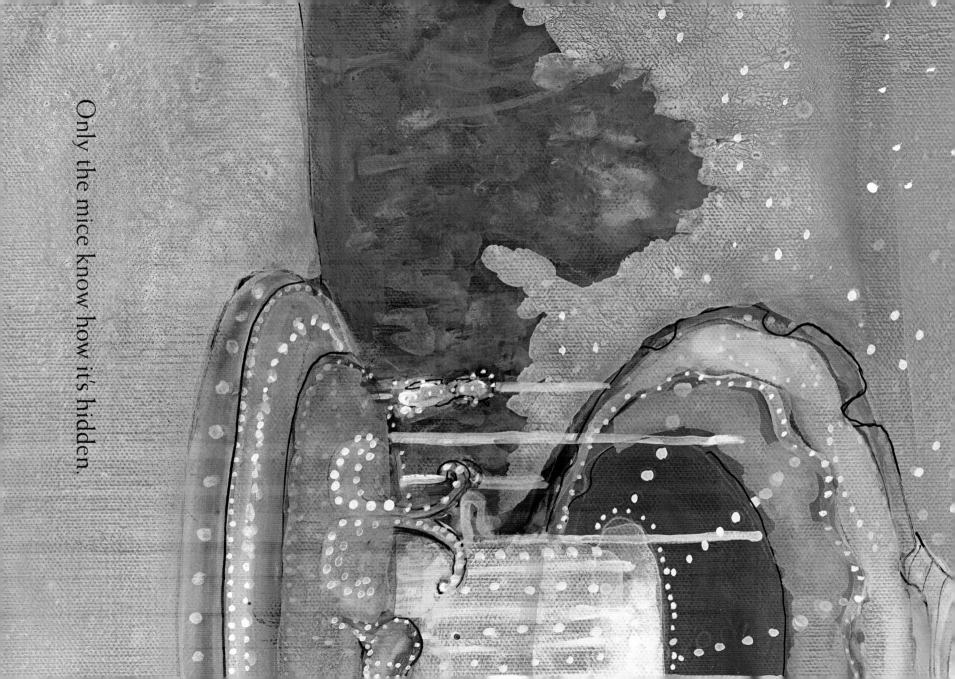

Only the mice know how it's hidden.

Only the mice know what to do there.

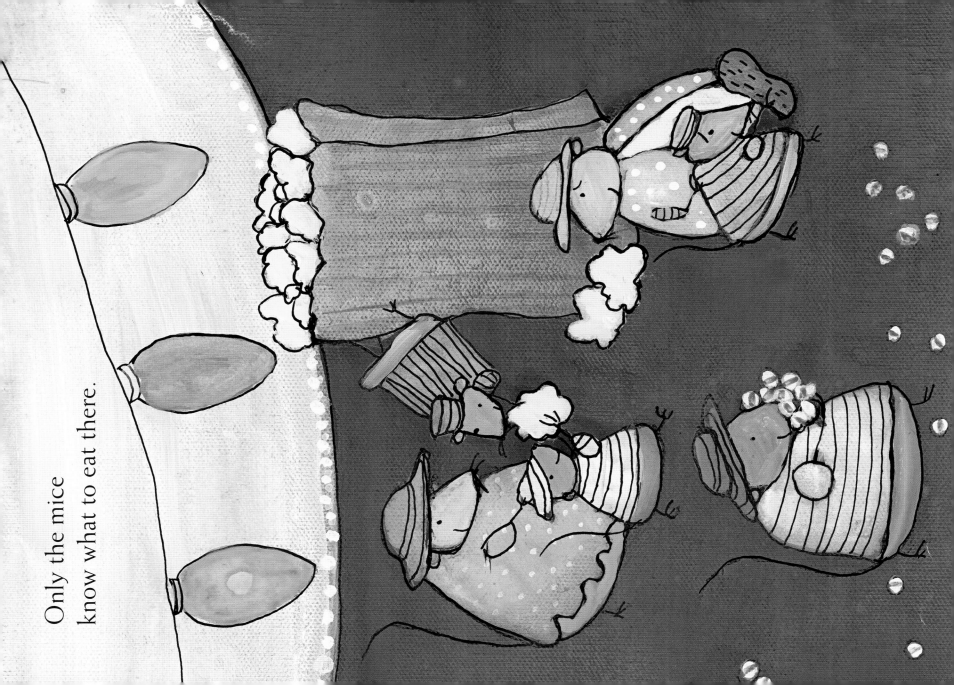

Only the mice
know what to eat there.

Only the mice know how to watch.

Only the mice know what they'll see there.

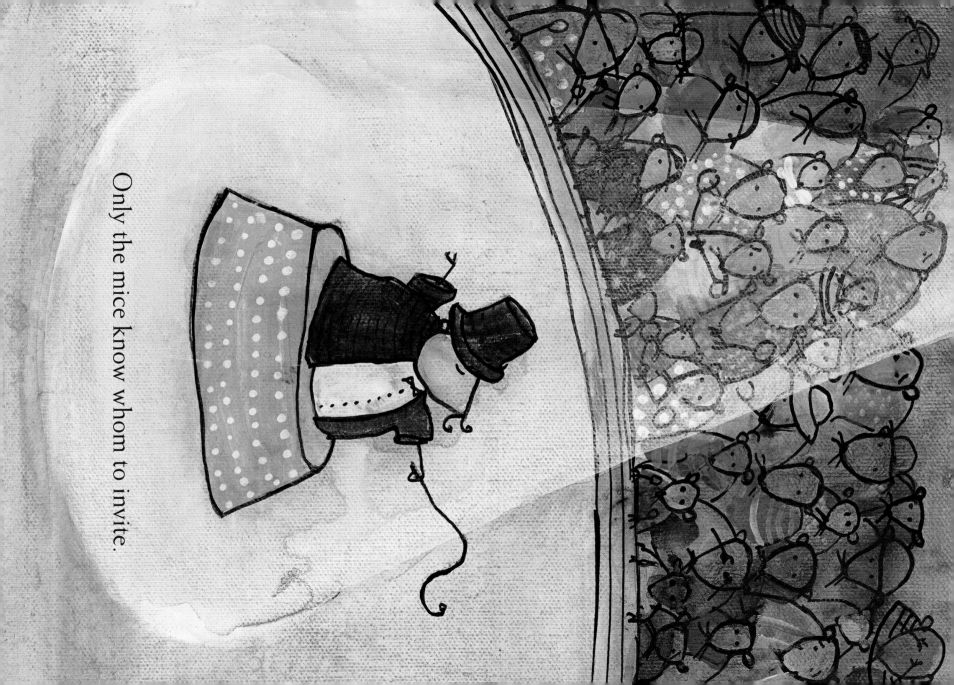

Only the mice know whom to invite.

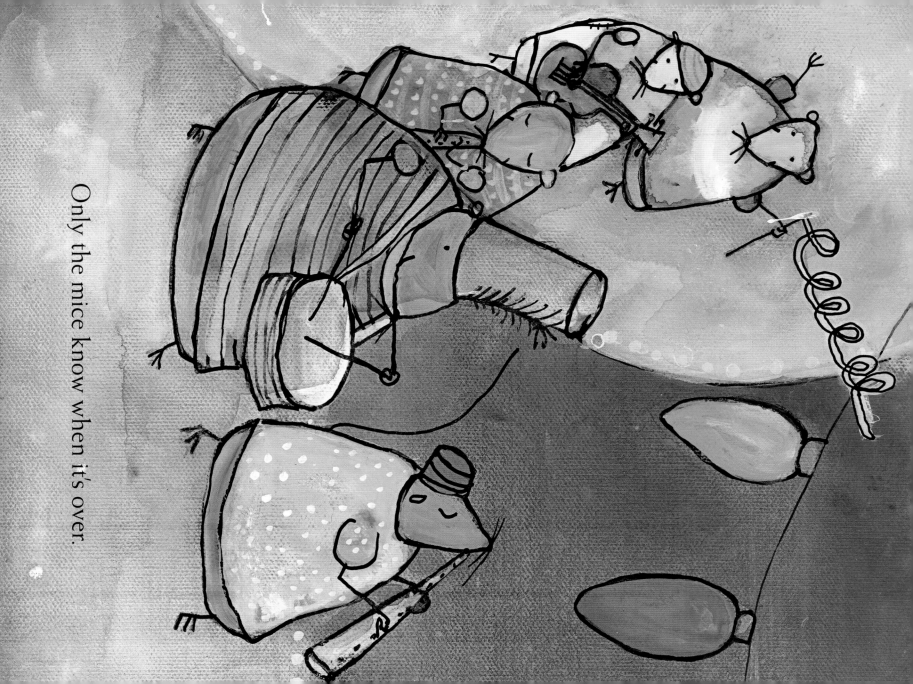

Only the mice know when it's over.

Only the mice know
how to keep the circus . . .

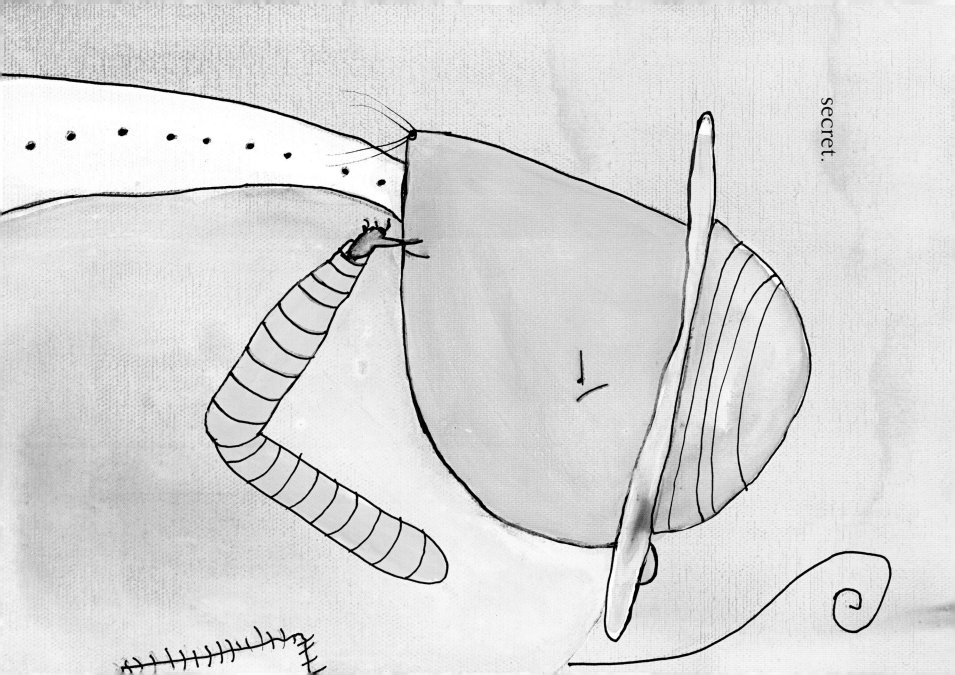

secret.